"For humans to have a responsible relationship to the world, they must imagine their places in it. To have a place, to live and belong in a place, to live from a place without destroying it, we must imagine it. By imagination we see it illuminated by its own unique character and by our love for it." — Wendell Berry

What If . . .

First English-language edition published in 2019 by Enchanted Lion Books
67 West Street, 317A, Brooklyn, NY 11222
Originally published in French in 2004 as Il Faudra
Copyright © 2004 by Éditions Sarbacane, Paris
English-language edition Copyright © 2019 by Enchanted Lion Books
Translation Copyright © 2019 by Enchanted Lion Books
All rights reserved under International and Pan-American Copyright Conventions
A CIP record is on file with the Library of Congress
ISBN: 978-1-59270-281-7
Printed in China by R. R. Donnelley Asia Printing Solutions, Ltd.
First Printing

What If . . .

Thierry Lenain   Olivier Tallec

Translated from the French by Claudia Zoe Bedrick

ENCHANTED LION BOOKS
NEW YORK

A child sat on his island,
looking out at the world and thinking.

The child saw war.
"We could paint over their uniforms,"
he thought.
"And turn their guns into bird perches
and shepherd's flutes."

The child saw famine.
"What if we lasso the clouds
and bring rain to the desert?
What if we dig rivers of water and milk?"

The child saw misery.
"We'd better learn to add, subtract, multiply, and
divide," he thought. "What if we finally learned
to share water, bread, air, and earth?"

The child saw the powerful gorging,
ordering, shouting, and decreeing.
And he said to himself, "We have
to open their eyes or drive them out."

The child looked out at the ocean and thought,
"What if we wash it clean?"
Then he sat in front of it, just dreaming.

The child saw forests.
He thought how great it would be to walk there,
exploring and telling stories to be carried on the wind.
Later, he'd fall asleep on the moss, listening.

The child saw tears.
"We have to hug," he decided,
"and not be afraid of kisses.
What if we start saying 'I love you,'
even if we've never heard it before?"

The child lowered his head.
He saw the moon with a flag stuck right in its face.
"How dumb," he thought, "to try to own the moon.
What if we set it free and say we're sorry?"

The child looked out at the world
from his island one last time.

Then he decided...

...to be born.

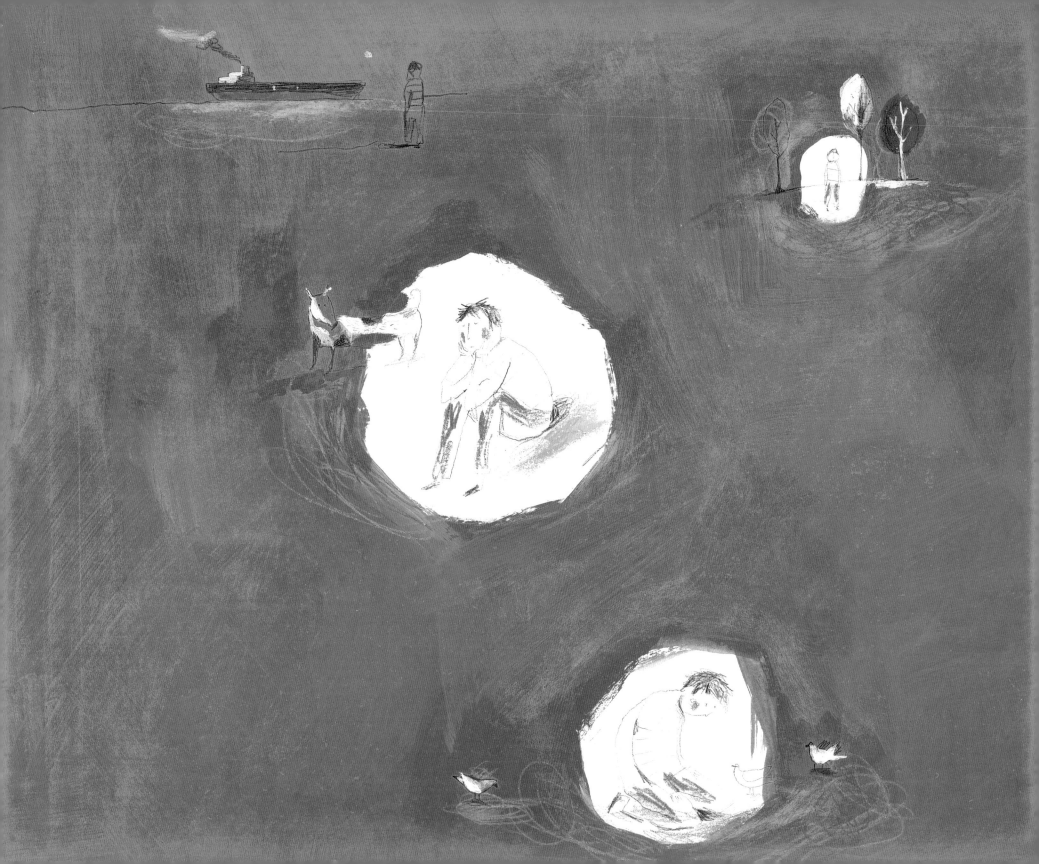